On the Way

A Collection of poems and photographs

Penny Villegas

Copyright © Penny Villegas.

All rights reserved. No part of this book may be reproduced in any form or by any electronic or mechanical means, including information storage and retrieval systems, without permission in writing from the publisher, except by reviewers, who may quote brief passages in a review.

ISBN: 978-1-63649-965-9   (Paperback Edition)
ISBN: 978-1-63649-966-6   (Hardcover Edition)
ISBN: 978-1-63649-964-2   (E-book Edition)

Some characters and events in this book are fictitious. Any similarity to real persons, living or dead, is coincidental and not intended by the author.

Book Ordering Information

Phone Number: 347-901-4929 or 347-901-4920
Email: info@globalsummithouse.com
Global Summit House
www.globalsummithouse.com

Printed in the United States of America

On the Way
A Collection of poems and photographs
By Penny Villegas

Biography of Penny Villegas

Born into a small farming community, I went to a one room country school --all 8 grades there. Since there were no school busses to take me to junior high, as we called it, or senior high, I went to live with my grandmother in Rock Island. These advanced schools had more than one thousand students, with wardrobes and vocabulary well beyond my country ways. I survived and then went to the Catholic women's college which teamed up with the Catholic men's college for parties. At one of these I met a handsome man from Colombia: we fell in love, our hearts melded in a love that would last 60 years. During these years, we had five children, we lived in Medellin, Colombia we lived in Columbia, Missouri, and we now live in Orlando, Florida. These years full of love and family were the settings for On The Way.

This book has aspects of both a novel, and a diary; a novel because of its setting and dramatic characters, a diary because as I lived in these two cities, I lived this story. My Heart is present throughout the story of the two families who lived so many years ago in Colombia and with their struggles with loss and love. The reader will also learn about Colombia, with scenes from a big city- Medellin- with a population nearing one million, mostly citypeople and their fancy automobiles and the countryside with barefoot campesinos walking on dirt roads and foot worn paths up the Andes mountains. Here, many characters, men and women, young and old, doctors and lawyers and campesinos live and die.

ACKNOWLEDGMENTS

The poem "Barren Signs" by Penny Villegas quotes the farmer's almanac in the publication THE FIDDLEHEAD published by the university of New Brunswick in Fredericton, New Brunswick. THE FIDDLEHEAD acknowledges the candidate council, university of New Brunswick, the Province of New Brunswick and St. Thomas University.

The poem "Leftovers" by Penny Villegas was published in the magazine MILDRED in the publication THE FIDDLEHEAD.

Thanks to Fernando Gutierrez whose help made this happen.

CONTENTS

In Naming We Love 1
My Mother 2
First Sight 3
This Was The Summer Of Our Learning 4
All The Stars Show 6
A Maying 7
In Spring 9
Call Daddy To The Phone 10
Villa 12
On Losing And Finding 13
Calypso, A Scarlet Macaw 15
The Harps 17
First Snow 19
Amigos 20
At The Children's Home 21
The Fledgling 22
Twenty Years Away 23
The Day We All Went Into The Sun 24
Savant 26
Tethered 27
Riddle 28
On The Other Side 29
The Year Of Stars 30
Spring At The Santa Fe River 32
The Drought In India 34
Choosing A Nest Site 35
Houdini Wish 36

Barren Signs 37
Leftovers.. 40
Litany 41
In Manizales 42
La Loca 43
Loss 44
Going Home 45
In The Sweat Lodge.. 47
In Spain 48
In Mourning 50
Recovered 51
At Payne's Pairie 52
Drought 54
November By The River 55
Flightless Birds... 58
The Woods 60

IN NAMING WE LOVE

The first love song was when Adam,
tired and alone among the damp clay beasts,
saw finally Eve: her dark doe's eyes,
her hair shining like a blackbird's wing,
her breasts, no other breasts like these--
(Oh, wings swept down his shoulders
and snakes slimmed up his spine--)
there were no breasts in the kingdom like these.
He sang as if all life depended upon it:
"Come closer, let me name you, closer,
come golden silk spider and green frog,
tether and tongue,
sing with me wrens and elephants,
trill and trumpet
the song of life God planted
the smile of the great ape,
in, oh the goodness of the Creator,
Woman."

MY MOTHER

My mother had a pair of hand-tooled leather, high-heeled, open-toed, ankle strap shoes she kept hidden in a box at the bottom of the dirty clothes hamper. Some days she would turn the radio up loud and come two-stepping out on the linoleum floor with her fancy shoes. I'd sit cross-legged under the table and feel the floor bounce and hear the tapping and watch her feet with red toenails in beautiful made-in-Mexico sandals fly by.

One night at a social at the schoolhouse someone stated to play old upright piano. Not Sing-along, but something that moved momma right out on the middle of the floor. Some man caught the bug who also knew how and they jitter-bugged past the school board, past farmers' wives in flour sack dresses, past the heavy sun burnt men whose foreheads and eyes showed white lily white. All the kids' mouths were clappering like the teacher's bell.
"Is that your mom?"
"yes," I said, "it is."

FIRST SIGHT

Sleepy still, Buddha-eyed,
no bigger than a few hours
or a man's hand—
her father's, for instance—
my son's. she is new,
her ears still pressed
outlined on her head.
Her mouth dreams of suck,
she wakes, her fingers
flutter like wings.
Her eyes, the color of deep water,
look through us, reflect us.
She raises her feather-fine eyebrows,
lifts the corners of her lips:
a smile, a butterfly.
Now I remember
when he was –ah, exactly this!

THIS WAS THE SUMMER OF OUR LEARNING

We watched them, our children,

A spun sugar bride and groom

On top a three-tiered cake.

Listening to their vows, we heard our own.

We cried for their beauty and their hopes,

Knowing that they hope, as we did,

for all the wrong things, but knowing,

as they do not yet, that the better will be learned

in tears, and the worse much worse

than they imagine.

And we gave thanks for our learning, at last,

That we are one.

We give thanks for each other:

good bread, a blessing and a staff.

A spun sugar bride and groom

ALL THE STARS SHOW

We are old star watchers,
Old friends. We loll on this
Hillside in a field of clover,
Another Milky Way.
Across the dark night sky,
The constellations pan;
We call them by name
With hushed cries, dove calls.
Suddenly, the stars begin to move
As steel shavings to a magnet;
They coalesce into new patterns,
Ragged fiery numbers, counting down:
605, 604, 603...
Until the edges of the sky
Tear loose, as a film from its reel,
Flapping, bleeding light.
We stagger to our feet and cry,
Shattered by the light,
"Let s hold hands now and rejoice.
The show is about to end."

A MAYING

My first corsage
for my first prom
was a gardenia
whose delicate
white petals
were so fragrant
they made me giddy.

Grandma warned me
my very breath
would bruise them.
she was right, but
it didn't stop me.
nothing could stop me.
It was my favorite flower
in those young days
and now I have
a full gardenia bush
in my backyard
with its flowers
--o many hundreds! –

all the young girls

in creamy blush

dying to open

into the day.

My first corsage for my first prom was a gardenia

IN SPRING

When the Confederate jasmine bloom
I remember Jeff Davis and
that idea-state whose end came
when flowers filled the air
and blood ran knee deep
in the field at Gettysburg.

And, on a smaller plain,
nearer and sweeter, but
no less death, I remember
the wreathes of jasmine and gardenia—
many hundreds more flowers
than the days of her life—
the wreathes of well wishers
sent to envelope our baby
and us as we stayed behind
in their perfume.

And still I would have
that perfume on the air.

CALL DADDY TO THE PHONE

He says he doesn't
Have anything to say.
Well, tell him I do.

What you want to waste your money for
Why is it a waste
I don't have a damn thing to say
I know
Then what you want to
I want to hear your voice
Oh
All these years I called Momma
sure that's right too
I never asked to talk to you
oh sure you did
not much I never thought
you wanted to talk
now you're talking crazy
(This is red alert)

We both cry

(The way he taught me

So no one else would know)

And I didn't say

It's not crazy

And I didn't say

I want to be crazy

I did say

I love you, Daddy.

VILLA

Whose old walls, thick as men's bodies,
Are made of mud: red clay kneaded,
Raised, smoothed by peasant hands,
Whitewashed inside and out.
These walls make home, hold us in, hold safe.

You can see in villages
These old houses fallen, left to be
The walls wash down, sprout green.
It is bliss to be grown again as grass.

ON LOSING AND FINDING

This is about how the eggs were warmed
those days the wrens couldn't find them,
when the painters moved the workbench,
the shovels and bikes, the rakes with old leaves impaled,
everything out of the garage.

On the second day, when our brooms caught at webs
and mud daubs fell, I saw the wrens, keeping distance.
On the third day, I found the nest,
a tangle of soft straw in a bucket of nails;
I placed it dead center of the angles the wrens flew.
Too late, too late, I said on the fourth day
as the wrens crisscrossed the space,
unseeing, bills open panting, or calling
some cry I could not hear.

Today, days since I last thought of them,
I see the wrens with worms; their freckled eggs
have hatched. The babies open broad yellow bills;
they regard me with veiled eyes.
As mine are, wondering again.

Are we not all warmed unawares?

As Tom was in his wrecked car?

As we, my dears, moved daily to love

despite it all.

CALYPSO, A SCARLET MACAW

She's an old bird, she's been around;
Once she lived in a chicken coop,
a jungle virago among the hens;
she learned to cackle and even crow. Now in her melancholy
moments, she nods, nodding, nodding as she clucks like a
broody hen mourning her lost chicks.
She must have lived in a bar too,
A low-down one where they'd keep a parrot
And teach it to swear, as she does
In several men's rough voices. One of them loved Lola; his
love lives on
In his call, the "oh" and the "ah" drawn into a promise. "Lola,"
The old bird calls in a baritone, "Loolaa."

Now Calypso lives in this patio, reliving all her past lives
And calling for her dinner, as the men here call Luisa!"
Hot days, the old lady brings a bucket of water,
And the macaw scrambles down from her perch.
She spreads her wings and her tail into fan,
A flamenco dancer's skirt in red and green,
as Luisa sprinkles water in the air.
The circle each other, calling one to the other
As the water falls in little rainbows on them both.

Calypso

THE HARPS

"Where's my Harps?" And Mom
would run while we kids stayed
still. My Dad would settle to his music
like a dog to sleep, going
around and around in some
space we could not see.
He'd cross his legs, sit forward in his chair,
his big work shoes,
with toes like turtle shells,
good for riding, poised.
Delivered his jew's harp,
he'd hold the metal bow of it,
study it, mouth it, nibble it,
settle it against his teeth.
His large clumsy freckled hands
would fall finally into grace,
into carved bowls to hold the music.
His hand and toe would spring
at once, at once to the song,
the jig, the march, the beat.
Warmed, he'd open the other case.

"This is a Hoehner," he'd say
reverently, whacking it against
His palm. Scowling, "somebody's
been messing with it." He
liked to hear it cry and pine
for the red River Valley
and the wings of angels, then
ease into the Strawberry Blonde;
by the time he got to Buffalo Gals,
his eyes were bright and Mom
was dancing double time.
We'd all get going good, then,
then
He'd end with a bark of laughter,
AHA!

FIRST SNOW

It was the quiet waked me,
And I waked you to see the strange light
Come filtered through the window,
A fern forest etched in ice
That melted in soft mouths into a new world.

The sky was just the color of a mourning dove's breast,
With quiet snow falling, almost static white,
Piled on black branches, heaped in soft hills
Over bruised grass.

We too are pale, quiet, reflecting that light,
and remember that poem—
"If a star were to fall,
I'd hold out my hand."

AMIGOS

We could see them
Old,
Mustachioed,
Black-hatted.
They held hands down the
Mountain road, and
Careened
In a steady unstoppable trot
To a swaying
Standstill.
Their conversation was intense.
They took turns giving
Attention, and
Embraces
To Balance and ballast
The other's path.

AT THE CHILDREN'S HOME

We scrubbed them three times the first day,
Sat them on our laps int the sun,
Combed their chick-fine hair for nits; We could not help
their alcoholic mother was dead.
They were orphaned or beaten or abandoned,
With more ways of suffering than I wanted to count,
As I counted the children who came,
their eyes darting like dark birds
flying against windows.
They refused smiles, speeches, intentions.
I would ask for a small hand,
Go to the big chair overlooking the lake, and
Lift that angled hesitation on my knee.
As I folded in my bones and hard edges,
I'd begin to hum, searching for the moment's note.
And soon the feet would stop running, kicking, twitching
Then the fists would open, the shoulders let down,
settle like wings.
We rock and do not speak. We rock and hum.

THE FLEDGLING

I set the baby on the board swing.
She perches, belly out,
feet curled up, hands tight round
the ropes,
she soars into the air.

Once the swinging begins,
she sings—not a baby's ululu—
but a clear sweet song:
I am a little winged one;
I fly up and they catch me
flying home.

TWENTY YEARS AWAY

I am stopped suddenly
in the shadow of a cloud
by the smell of a field
of alfalfa in full sun,
the sweet smell of fresh sweat;
the breath of a lover
washes in waves over me –
held again in August.
it will rain tiny frogs,
dark drops dancing.
Night will creep up to my ears,
and I will get one wish:
A glimpse of the lily
becoming flesh
and its full embrace

THE DAY WE ALL WENT INTO THE SUN

As far as I could see
I could see
cobwebs strung through the grass
like silver threads
I closed my eyes and
the sun through my eyelids
those veined lenses
red to orange to gold was
a bridge from my sight to the earth
And tripping from my tongue
came first a little black dog
leaping the mountain tops
shaking the orange trees and brown leaves
tumbling down also many children
thin shy ones and babies patting their fat hands
and my grandmother smiles at them
her hands folded in her apron
last rumbling and slow comes the great bear
and an old man with a straggly beard
All stand in that blinding mountain sun
blinking a bit but glad.

Only these saw how

the flurry of yellow leaves sent rattling

by the wind, turned with a flourish

into a flock of small golden birds

that flew back up up up

SAVANT

His real mother left him in a bin:
His new mother carried him on her back
Until his feet dragged on the ground.
He did not learn
To sit or speak.

When he was ten and larger than they,
His mama and papa propped his great soft bulk
between them both and taught him to walk.

Years later they are wakened
by his playing "Rhapsody in Blue" on the old upright
in their living room.
All day he listens to music;
all night he plays it.
His little mama shaves him, his papa walks him around the yard.
At age thirty he does not speak,
but he sings bel canto.
His round pale face upturned,
His blind eyes weeping. Why?
"Hallelujah" he sings in perfect pitch.
Amen, we sing, amen, amen.

TETHERED

Oh God,

I run to you to confess that though in this world of flesh

You are my dearest life,

I dream of bodies: lips, hands, smiles, yes, touch.

How much heaven there is in a body

Only intimacy tells.

The jugular bliss

We chance is for the moment

When God and I and the other

Meet--

(God keep us but do not keep us apart!)

RIDDLE

La necesidad tiene cara de perro: Old Spanish saying

Necessity,
As they say in Spanish
Has the face of a dog
Meaning teeth and therefore hunger
Mine say chomping
Like the grasshopper mouse
Who chases and chews
Down to nubbins still
finally, still (these teeth sound like castanets)

Or the garden snake whose crescent moon teeth hold her prey impaled--
Once I saw a toad scrambling with his front feet and
--swelling up he thought too much for death
but teeth and hunger won again
(the quiet was immense)
What I want to know is
That shadow that gnaws at my heels
And grows daily smaller—
Is it my life or my death?

ON THE OTHER SIDE

This mountain has a darkness seen only in dreams
And a pull downward not even trees can resist,
All paths disappear, the sky seeps away, the hiker
Becomes heavy, clambering over time-charred
Branchless giants fallen hemlocks pointing down.
The bears of this mountain are enchanted too
They do not hunt honey or barberries but wait like
Buddhas for those who leave the campfires and cabins
To climb long hours in the falling dark,
Who come finally to wait, fierce lovers in dream skins,
Sitting on the flat-topped rock, smiling into the teeth
That flash like falling stars.

THE YEAR OF STARS

I read an account of a time in the Middle Ages when
there was an unprecedented meteor shower that lasted for a month.
It was so fiery that nights were as bright as day.

Once the stars fell
a thousand an hour.
Such terror and such light!

Only God knows how many
Eyes scanned the night sky
And read the stars raining
Down as a sign of His might
Or His anger or His fall.

The ancients remembered that year
as the year of stars.
I have known such
plenitude of tears,
And though tonight
The calm sky is reflected

In my eyes,

and all the stars blink back unmoved,

I know those unfallen

Are infinite and bright.

SPRING AT THE SANTA FE RIVER

The Santa Fe River seems like all Southern rivers:

Tea colored, slow fringed by cypress—

But I wonder who would name a river Holy Faith and if their life went like mine.

The large river goes suddenly underground;

It disappears in the time spent enjoying the roundness,

how it pools there and the algae gathers,

and then,

no whirlpool, no dropping off,

just swamp and then dry land

and the river is gone.

Trees grow here and alligators as dark as mud

and as toothed as the palmetto and pink flowers

that smell sweeter than any other spring.

There are clues

For those who, looking back, see how the river

begins to run faster and faster: how it dimples—

no white water—just the sureness when the undercurrent

swirls and mouths the air.

It leaps and circles before the dark sink.

Three miles later, if you can follow them,

If you can be a dousing stick and follow the great river

as it flows underneath, if you can make do with the air

  And the green, the Santa Fe will surface and seem

    to be again a river like any other Southern river.

Before the sink: a graveyard littered with lumbers,

Washed trunks, all the large things that cannot dive.

THE DROUGHT IN INDIA

In the Ghia Forest of India
A herder climbs trees and pulls
Down the topmost branches,
The last bit of green anywhere,
For his buffalo who have been
Watching heaven too long.
The herder's son watches;
He has one silver earring
And large black eyes that see
And find it clear that
This is forest: all dust
And the leaves of the trees
Out of reach.
Later, later
The lions lie down at the buffalo's
flank, nuzzle there
the warmth and knead the fawn belly.
It is a love feast.
They close their eyes.

CHOOSING A NEST SITE

The wren and I faced off
again this spring.
She scolds me,
Thinks my heavy moving
A mountain
to her lightning wings,
her mother's needs.

I think I'll match her will
This year—as I remember
Those four fat fledglings, saucy gifts to air,
brought down by my dogs

HOUDINI WISH

Not every day but some days of some weeks
Life's hard edges spring up around me
Pinch me like the walls of steamer trunks
My skin is a strait jacket
Tied with my past
The breath I long for is everywhere
If the handcuffs of my heart
Would break
I would fly
Like the light from sun
To everywhere
and everywhere would be home

BARREN SIGNS

Never plant anything in barren signs. They are good only for grubbing, trimming, and destroying noxious growth."
The Farmers' Almanac

Since he was beyond our help or our sight,
we carried our grief to the land

To work to be done; blessed certainties,
nails to be driven, ground to be turned,

Buckets of water to be dipped from the stream
and carried spilling upland.

The Almanac warned against planting and
though we ached to plant a tree for him,

it seemed a good time to listen and learn so
we took our hoes and forked spades

to bury some part of him and us

clearing the undergrowth for the garden.

The wild raspberries had been hacked off so often that under

earth was a seamed and solid patch of roots,

a network of scars

knotting, then diving deeper to wedge in clumps.

Survivors,

these brambles have slender thorny branches
above ropey roots

that zigzag across the field; they are hung with hearts, meat-colored and stunted,

woody tubers that hold on after the root is gone.

This saves it, of course.

We knew it would not be easy.

What else did we learn?

That tears taste the same as sweat,

That crying is hard work but digging helps,
that holes once dug

Take long times to fill.

That days pass.

We looked at the field of roots, and at each other's empty eyes

And we felt like Adam and Eve with God the Father standing on the other side

Of what might have been

And what was.

LEFTOVERS

We who would mother every single thing in the world
Not just living things
Or even lovely things but broken things
Discarded things and remembering the hungry
Even two spoonsful of casserole
must be eaten or wrapped.

Believing that nothing should go
Unwanted unloved unmourned
We are
Sometimes weighed down
By so many children we don't know what to do
And it's getting harder to laugh as we go on
our kids gone or grown
some friends already dead,
some lost
we must hold tight
and pray with all our might
we will not be left (dear God)
alone

LITANY

Her broom sends dust in whispered volleys;
Feathers fly, then float and settle back under the canaries
'cages.
Little storms of silence
Cloud the patio as she passes.
The grizzled dog groans and moves
From under the beds where she reaches
The coarse black nests of his hair.

The old lady, her long hair tumbling from its bun
From so many bows to low beds,
So many recalcitrant corners,
Keeps time. Prays for mercy. Her broom
Stirs a whirlwind of old down and dust;
Our dust, our wearing away, surrounds her,
And us all, like a prayer.

IN MANIZALES

Dios Misericordioso
allowed the beggarman
another day.
His grey head wheel high
to the cars that rushed around him,
he inched
with turtled intensity,
across the intersection.

Lifting his domed body,
dragging hi limp legs,
he defied gravity, drunk drivers,
belief.
I jangled coins into his palm.
He gave me, not thanks,
but promises of heaven
and a smile that split the sky.

LA LOCA

She wears layer upon layer of black, the mourning of years, torn open many places to another black, stained and crusted.

The Blackest Black is her eyes, bright as beasts's.

He hair a coarse nest—for cuckoos or cucarachas shout the town boys who run after to touch her rags, shout Loca in her face.

Her great grandson moves into her skirts;

He stands like a crane on one thin leg

As she hurls rocks, curses, horse manure.

She dumps her daily load of trash in front of her hut.

She lives by this and a son's occasional charity.

Old papers and bottles. Old clothes. Cigarette butts.

Her face collapses in the concentration of brushing tobacco, smoothing thin papers.

Sometimes I give her a cigarette.

Her face creases, the star of one tooth appears in her smile.

The little boy peers out at me, studies her, put his thumb in his mouth. They both suck contentedly.

LOSS

My woods, my weed patch,

My sea of straw,

Of foxtails, of elderberry

Of brambles

All that was

And was never mine

Is gone.

One morning

A bulldozer began

And dug in my stomach

All day. Not a leaf of green remains.

The night sky is

A pall, a low dun drape

Covering the earth.

The soft shrill

calls of bats

are like silk

shredding.

GOING HOME

Leaving, you see, I was
so sure, so ferocious
I ran, as the fox must after
freeing herself from the trap,
after turning her teeth
to herself.
how could I limp,
flying?

after thirty years
I stop in a sweat.
I am on the old road,
seen twice larger
through the lens of years.
I see charred shadows
where something ended,
limbs outstretched. Further,
strangely blocked, the road
is strewn, not by boulders,
but large noble beasts:
moose, elk, bear

sprawl in fixed deaths

In the way I must go.

(They do not blame me;

Their eyes are soft and unseeing.)

IN THE SWEAT LODGE

The first rock split open

Sky Earth

Standing Eagle threw sage on the stones

Bringing the desert to burn with us.

He brushed them with a twist of sweetgrass and

Prairies rose before us.

The dipper poured water on the stones:

Water marries fire; flaming starts rise.

We, weighed down by many burdens bodies past,

Are melted down to earth, down to stones,

Down through open eyes

Streaming into one dark we sing.

We are lost in old words old promises

Made before time before light before words.

Listen to the rocks.

Feed the fire with tobacco. It too has a song and

The Sweetgrass that traces a path through the night.

Remember the stone that split?

How its perfect halves each burned?

So do we.

So do we.

IN SPAIN

In the museum of religious art
Hang crucifixes of gold
And wood and stone
hang jesuses he
dies a thousand deaths
each detailed in pain
and the artists with
grim faithfulness
picture blood drip
run spurt pool
and as the agony comes
true to our everyday skin
and bones break
eyes fill: here is art
so every minute of every day
we remember sin

but I watch
those outstretched arms
stretch up and through that
last skin between the worlds

the fingers reach into feathers

and gather force

his word filled

the cup that was his life

until it shattered

some say the sky grew black

some could see

his flight and be glad

if I could be somebody

in this world of pain I would say free him

from his cross I would say

he is risen and you can too. A thousand thousand angels

with downy nets of light

wait for the moment when

remembering that the hold

of the world is slight

we fly

IN MOURNING

She looked up
past me, past the pine tree
past the stars
and I knew she would never stop
seeing what she saw
and then she was gone
Amen amen
but Mother
the mother
is our first world
our earliest earth
we draw our bones
from her bones and teeth
and our flesh from her

Dust and ashes

Dust and ashes
Amen
although it's not
only ashes and tears
my eyes are dry
but my body aches
for her

RECOVERED

The second time Tom learned to talk
He began again with Mama.
He had to learn to walk too;
First on two crutches; then on one.
See how he lists as he moves, away
From the car that hit him,
Tacking into a better wind.

His Indian hair grows in surprised spurts
Around his scars; he leans
 into his good ear, eagerness and caution meet.
 He's almost well; he's almost new;
There's a sweetness in him beyond
His twenty-five years, past his recovering.
It says, I was dead, but now I live

AT PAYNE'S PAIRIE

Long-limbed live oaks sprawl
Across the budding brush of March.
The sweet green stars of the gum tree
Thrust along with the palmetto's bold hands
Right to the edge of the prairie.
Waves of color and the hum of
A million bright-winged insects
Took our city wits and sent them tumbling

A tree fell. So near our hearts stopped,
Rabbits at its first snap.
All things stopped for its ponderous
Down coming; it crashed and resounded
Against those who remained standing.
Shaken,
we start up the tower: three tiers
to the sky and at each landing
hush. Housetop high at least,
eye level to the sky, the tree tops
sway, and so do we, green sailors in this sea.

The horizon, our equator surrounds us.
The prairie is a green sky with clouds of
Pink phlox, yellow grassy rains blowing,
Bare bushes rising grey in fog and mist
   Along the river, sky flung silver.

The hawks sweep low: two still shadows
Falling north. Egrets lift from the reeds,
One by white one to their night's place.
   Little birds in fives and sixes--
Wings flicker and stop, flicker and stop—
   Weave grace notes into summer.

The heron, old hermit, slow flapper,
   Leads into a tarnished silver sky,
   Down the creaking stairs to dusk.
We step over the log, the tree that fell,
   At one already with the mound
   Where the violets grow.

DROUGHT

A herder in the Ghia forest
in India climbs trees
and pulls down
the topmost branch,
the last bit of green in the sky,
for his buffalo, who have been,
in the way of cattle everywhere,
waiting patiently.

We do not see the herder's wife but
his son has one silver earring
and large black eyes
that see and therefore now
that a forest is thus: dust
with tree leaves hard picking.

The lions lie down
at the buffalo's flank,
nuzzle there the warmth,
knead the fawn bely.
It is a love feast.
They close their eyes.

NOVEMBER BY THE RIVER

I.

The Carnival colors are gone.

The leaves now are people-colored,

with branches faded too

to the color of an old face.

Two men sit in front of their tin-patched house—

the road cut it out from under them almost—

but, patched too, they hunker there

and smile riddling smiles

and wave pink palms.

Dark pink as the fields above the bluff,

and the leaves now clatter

above the silent water;

the river shines cobalt, yellow,

pink in leaves and waves of water.

II.

We lie on a barge with the grit of sand,

smell of rust and river, still and heavy

but still feel the water moving under us.
Watch the waves,
the colors melt and fuse, swirling into deep.
Pale surfaces belly into black.

III.
Quiet, quiet, until
the leaves, creased sepia—
like faces smiling in the sun—
bowed on stems from bending in the wind,
begin to clatter.

Those teeth won't catch us,
nor the hawk, red tail fanned,
wings bowed into the wind
to be still. Buoyed there
for a moment
before turning and curving down.

None of these.
Tristeza, Felicidad: black Orpheus go down,
down, down you hawk, you devil, god,
You-me.

IV.

The bluffs are white, the field palm warm.

Some gather there

and roused from their music

wave at us so far below.

FLIGHTLESS BIRDS

On some exotic island,
Borneo or Papua or Fiji,
they've discovered
one last hope, that is, a hen
of this particular species of parrot.

Green, owl-sized, upright,
called good natured by scientists
who counted six in the whole world,
all males that gather daily
to drum short wings in the dust
and drone in the dusk
to attract a female—
Which after ten years appeared,
without getting sentimental,
the scientific community
announced the answer to prayers
of bird lovers everywhere.
Only the six old birds who
still drum daily are not surprised.
Now there is a chick

after perhaps forty years
of no chicks of this feather,
science took a camera in its nest;
it totters around chirruping,
messing, pecking here and there
under the roots of a tree.
It's waiting for its mother;
two miles she walks for the fruit
her chick eats, she fills her gullet and walks back again.
You see the absurdity of it;
the chick alone in a hole,
the old males still drumming—
it happened once, maybe it will again–
the mother walking, walking,
just one foot in front of the other,
while cats, tame tabbies
turned out for the night
Prowl.

THE WOODS

Today I sat where I had not sat before

in the old rocker, its arms worn free

of paint, and I sat where he had sat so many times

and I saw what he had seen over and over and over:

The woods. Oak trees, pine trees, maple and behind these familiar were unknown trees in green

just green woods

and I rocked as he had rocked, the steady tock to the ever-present tick, tick tock tick tock

and I watched the woods as he had watched the trees he knew and the many more he did not know

Nor what lay beyond

and wondered as he had—What now what now what now

Now, now, now

and then he left me with the rocker and the tock and my own

what now

www.ingramcontent.com/pod-product-compliance
Lightning Source LLC
LaVergne TN
LVHW051226070526
838200LV00057B/4625